# Part Three

## To Prevent Clear Paths

# Emily Martha Sorensen

# To Prevent Clear Paths

To Frederik Vendelin,

longtime fan of the comic,
reader of my other books,
and Patreon supporter.

# Chapter 1
## The Downstairs

Following Kendra down into the dungeons, Chronos was in a rather sour mood. She reflected on the past few days and wondered what, exactly, she was supposed to have done to deserve this.

"Always read your contracts before you sign!" Kendra called in a singsong voice as she skipped down the stairs two at a time.

*Other than that,* Chronos thought grumpily.

Lining each of the long walls below her was a long row of ten cages. They were classic steel bars, very sturdy, clearly intended for holding one or possibly more crowded prisoners in each. Perfect for a villain who meant to keep many people restrained. Except for one small, pesky detail: all the steel bars in between the cages had been removed, which meant that each row was more like one long, enormous cage.

Oh, yes, and the locks on all of the cage doors were missing.

Clutter crowded everywhere. There were cute little girl outfits flung all over the floor, dirty dishes in stacks of plates, bits of gears and tools, posters papering the walls, and many other esoteric things that were most likely magical technology imported from other worlds. There was also an ordinary-looking refrigerator parked against the short wall at the far end, incongruously.

"So *these* are the dungeons," Chronos muttered, looking around on her way down the stairs.

A little blonde head popped up from behind a tall box. It belonged to a small girl who looked about ten, with fluffy pigtails dangling from each side of her head.

"Oh, is Baron Deathwave dead?" the girl asked matter-of-factly. "Are you my new masters?"

Chronos was unsure of how to respond to that. "I . . . suppose . . ."

The little girl clapped her hands, her pigtails bobbing. "I haven't had a girl master since Dusk Anesthesia got thrown in prison! I hope you'll be nicer than she was! She never wanted to play with me and she told me to stop talking. Do you want to meet my new brainwasher? I named him Brian!"

"Brainwasher," Chronos said flatly.

*Is this actually a prisoner?* she wondered. *Or was this a minion?*

"How can you live in this dump?!" Kendra burst out.

Chronos glanced in her direction. The former magical girl was staring at the piles of clutter and mess in clear horror.

The prisoner-who-was-possibly-a-minion seemed to take this as a request for a tour. She hopped to her feet and pointed eagerly all over the room. "Well, there's a bathroom over there, I sleep in this cell here, I get my food from there . . ."

"A refrigerator," Kendra said flatly, standing in front of the incongruous furnishing.

"A refrigerator that automatically restocks itself from nearby grocery stores!" the little girl cried, waving her hands excitedly.

"Does the refrigerator also *pay* for the food it takes?" Chronos asked suspiciously.

The little girl opened her mouth to answer, and then she paused. Her eyes flicked from one side to the other. "I didn't design it!"

*Terrific,* Chronos thought. *That's another point in favor of "minion." She's clearly an accomplice in thievery.*

It would be bad enough to inherit somebody else's prisoner, but somebody else's minion . . . that would be far more difficult to get rid of, and you'd have to worry about previous loyalties.

# The Downstairs

She had been starting to consider maybe staying, but this clinched it. There was no way she was going to deal with *two* unwanted minions when she didn't even want to be a villain in the first place.

Kendra would have been bad enough. The fact that the former magical girl did not take no for an answer would not have boded well for her obeying someone she claimed she wanted as a boss. But this certainly tipped the balance.

"Kendra's your new master," Chronos said, turning to walk back up the stairs. "Listen to whatever she says. I'm leaving."

"Hang on!" Kendra shouted indignantly. "Did you not hear what I said about not being able to lead a new team?!"

Chronos shrugged and started heading upward.

Kendra teleported right in her path.

Chronos sighed heavily. *I should definitely never have given her that watch.*

"Ooh, do you have teleporting magic?" the little girl squealed from downstairs. "I wish I could do that! I would have gotten out of here aaaaaaaaages ago!"

Reluctantly, her path blocked, Chronos turned around and trudged back down the stairs. Kendra followed close behind her.

"I've been here for yeaaaaaaaaaars," the little girl announced, flinging her arms wide. "Nobody ever lets me out. It's really boring!"

"I wonder why," Kendra said, her voice heavy with irony. "Could it be because you're a prisoner?"

The little girl pouted. "I try to be useful. I try! But nobody ever lets me out! They're so mean!"

Chronos revised her opinion again. *Prisoner. Prisoner who just wants to go home and is trying to make the best of a bad situation.* She was starting to feel sorry for the kid.

"Are you a born mage?" the little girl asked in a wistful tone. "I've always wanted to be a born mage. Then I could keep my magic forever."

*Ha!* Chronos thought. *It's not as appealing as it sounds!*

"No," Kendra said shortly. "It's magical technology."

"It's the watch," Chronos added, pointing at Kendra's wrist.

Kendra gave her a heavy glare.

*What?* Chronos thought. *Was she trying to keep it a secret?*

"Ooh, I love magical technology!" the girl squealed. "Can I see can I see can I see?!"

She bounced forward, but Kendra's spiked halo was in her hand and pointed at the little girl's face in a flash.

The prisoner pouted. "I just wanted to seeeeeeeee!"

"No touching," Kendra snapped. "Stay back. Stay over there!"

*That's a little harshly to treat a kid, isn't it?* Chronos thought, wondering what the problem was with the former magical girl. She shook her head.

"Can I maybe upgrade it later?" the little girl asked hopefully from her spot several feet away. A wand with a pink heart on top and many ribbons spiraling underneath appeared in her hand. "I'm very good at upgrading things. They usually still work afterwards!"

"Stay . . . over . . . there," Kendra growled.

"I can fix it if it breaks, too!" the little girl said excitedly. "Just watch! BREAK IT!"

A shattering sound came from Kendra's wrist. Shards of glass *tink*ed quietly to the concrete floor beneath them.

Kendra stared at her wrist in aghast horror.

"FIX IT!" the little girl cried, pointing her wand again.

The watch was immediately good as new.

*"Never do that again!"* Kendra roared.

Chronos silently cursed herself for not taking the opportunity to escape while she could have. But this raised intriguing possibilities for the future. If all she had to do was to convince the little girl to break the watch and never fix it again, that would be the perfect solution to ditch her unwanted stalker of a former magical girl.

Assuming that Kendra couldn't find a way to fix it afterwards.

"You needed to *see*," the little girl said, as if that were obvious.

Chronos frowned. *Why in the world didn't she just break the walls of the dungeons if she wanted to escape and get back home that badly?* It didn't quite make sense that someone who had the power to break things could be held prisoner. She felt like she was missing something.

"Can you only use that power a few times a day?" Chronos asked.

"No," the little girl said. "I can use it whenever I want."

"Can you only use it on magical things?" Chronos hedged.

"No," the little girl said proudly. "I can fix and break anything."

"Then why are you still a prisoner here?!" Kendra expostulated. "You could have escaped anytime!"

The little girl stared at her blankly. "Where would I go?"

*Of course,* Chronos realized. *She doesn't know which way her home is. How could she? On top of that, there's no easy way to transport to and from this lair if you can't drive. We're not exactly in a populated area.*

A plan was starting to form in Chronos's mind. It was a pretty devious plan, for Chronos. She would ask Kendra to teleport the little girl home, and then the little girl could break the watch while Kendra was there. Then all that had to happen was that no one fixed the watch, and Chronos would be free. It was the perfect idea.

"Kendra," Chronos said, "can you take her back ho—"

"No," Kendra said immediately.

"Then I'll take her ba—" Chronos began, holding out her hand for the watch.

"Do you think I'm stupid?!" Kendra asked incredulously.

There seemed to be a slight wrinkle in the perfect plan.

"What *are* you, anyway?" Kendra demanded, whirling on the prisoner. "A magical girl?'

"Actually . . . I dunno." The little girl put a finger to her mouth, tapping it thoughtfully. "I haven't transformed in years."

"Have you *tried?*" Kendra asked.

The little girl shrugged. "It doesn't work anymore."

"Then you're probably a verge," Chronos said.

"A whaaat?" the little girl asked. Her mouth opened in bafflement.

"A verge," Chronos said. "It's short for 'on the verge of losing magic.' It refers to a magical girl who can't transform anymore, but still retains some of her powers. Like Kendra."

"Wrong," Kendra said.

"That's why you still have the ability to fix and break things," Chronos explained. "Kendra still has some of her powers, too."

"Wrong," Kendra said.

"Of course, you won't have any powers you used to have to transform to use, which is why Kendra being a verge isn't as obvious, but in your case —"

"Stop calling me that!" Kendra exploded. "I defected!"

"Yes," Chronos said dryly. "In order to save the world."

"That doesn't matter!" Kendra screamed. "My powers are *gone!*"

Chronos glanced down at the spiked weapon in the annoying lunatic's hand. "Then how come you still have your halo?"

Kendra started to speak. She stopped. She started to speak. She stopped. She stared at the spiky halo with huge eyes.

"Right," Chronos said. "If you'd quit, it would have crumbled. Instead, it changed form. I'm guessing you can't transform any longer, but it's possible you still can. If you just go back home —"

"No!" Kendra shouted.

Chronos sighed.

"No," Kendra grated, squeezing the golden halo with each of her fingers between two spikes. "I can't go back home. I have to stop that future."

Chronos started to speak, to remind her with exasperation that that future was, in fact, gone — but then a shiver ran down her back.

*I can't see any futures I'm involved in. How do I know whether that future really is gone forever, or whether it's only missing from my power because I would now be mixed up in it?*

It was a horrifying thought, and she could find no comforting certainties to lean on as reassurances.

She'd thought she'd stopped Cream Angel from changing into the frightening Avenging Angel forever. But what if she'd just triggered Avenging Angel's existence in another way?

*I have to get away from Kendra,* Chronos thought, her heart racing. *I have to be so far removed that her futures will be clear to my sight again. Only then can I be sure we'll be safe.*

But how could she do that when the former magical girl was determined to involve her in every possible future? Even if she *did* manage it, how could she ever be sure?

"Maybe you should try to transform," Chronos said. "Maybe we should find out for sure."

"No," Kendra said. Her knuckles were white as she squeezed the golden halo in the places between the spikes. "My magic is gone. I've never had powers I could use while not transformed. I never saw the point."

"*I* saw the point," the little girl said. "My masters always said to stop transforming because it was really loud and took forever and it drove them crazy —"

"So what does it really matter?" Kendra went on, talking over top of her. "So I'm a verge. So what? What does it really *mean?* Nothing. It means nothing, that's what."

She gripped the halo even more tightly. She didn't even seem to notice that the spikes were digging into her flesh.

*It means that you can summon your focus item,* Chronos thought. *It means that any powers it had, it probably still does. That's not nothing.*

She wasn't sure if Kendra's focus item was an heirloom. Probably not — but if it had once belonged to another magical girl, and been passed along to a new one before the original had lost her powers, it would permanently retain some of the magic from the original magical girl. Heirloom focus items were uncommon in the West, but they were considered highly desirable in Africa and Asia.

"Did your focus item itself have any powers?" Chronos asked.

"Boomerang," Kendra said tensely. "It always came back to my hand, even if I didn't actively summon it."

"See if it still does," Chronos said.

Kendra hesitated, but she threw back her arm and flung the halo across the room. It whirled in a bladed blur, swished in an arc, and whooshed back to Kendra's waiting hand.

"*Ouch!*" Kendra shouted. She held up her hand, which had a mild slice across her palm. "Stupid villain weapon!"

Chronos bit back a snort of amusement. This wasn't the first time she had seen a villain injured by their own spikes.

"FIX IT!" the little girl said hopefully, but the hand didn't heal. A line of blood welled up from Kendra's palm.

"I take it that's not a healing power," Kendra said acidly, squeezing her hand into a fist to stop the bleeding.

"It used to be, when I could transform," the little girl said sadly.

"It's fine," Kendra snapped, squeezing her hand tightly. "I'm fine. It's no big deal. I'll find a bandage or something."

"Oh, Bailey the Band-Aid Box is over there," the little girl said, pointing.

Kendra marched off in that direction, her lips set in a grim line, not looking particularly hopeful at her chances of finding the item in this huge mess. That left Chronos alone with the prisoner. She tried to think of a topic of conversation.

"Did anyone ever try to get ransom for you?" Chronos asked at last. She was wondering why the kid was still here, if she'd been here for years.

"Strykewell Strykefast tried!" the little girl said. "He accidentally got killed by his own gun."

"Nobody else?" Chronos asked.

"Dusk Anesthesia threatened to, but then she accidentally got caught and thrown in prison."

A chill ran down Chronos's spine. She had a rising sense of misgiving that those two accidents hadn't been accidents. "So why have your previous . . . owners kept you alive?"

"'Cause I build great weapons, and I'm only slightly annoying!" the little girl announced proudly.

"You supply *villains* with *weapons*?" Kendra roared, marching back towards them. She now had five or six band-aids plastered across her hand.

The little girl shrunk away. "The first one asked nicely!"

"Kendra . . . she's been raised by villains," Chronos said. "Of course she's corrupt."

"I'm not corrupt!" the little girl exclaimed, her voice rising in high-pitched horror.

Kendra turned and gave the little girl a flat stare.

Chronos, who was starting to get suspicious, did the same.

The little girl's eyes filled with tears, and she sniffled pitifully. She held out her hands in a plea of abject misery.

Both flat stares continued.

"Well, all right, maybe," the little girl conceded, pinching her fingers together. "Just a little. A smidge. A teensy-weensy, tiny-winy, itty-bitty smidge —"

"You *built* a *brainwasher!*" Kendra shouted.

"It *sounded* like *fun!*" the little girl defended.

Chronos clutched her forehead. *Help* . . .

# Chapter 2
## The Lunchroom

Looking around the lunchroom, Florence's stomach lurched to see Felicity at their usual table, opening a brown paper sack.

*How can she sit there?* Florence wondered. *How can she sit there without Kendra?*

The most impossible thing in the world had happened — Kendra had quit being a magical girl. Not only that, she had quit before either of them, in such a mind-bogglingly insane way that it make any sense in Florence's head.

Why had Kendra done that? Why had Kendra *left?* Where *was* Kendra, anyway?

Florence's grip tightened on her lunch tray. She breathed in and out.

*It's been three days,* she told herself. *If Felicity can act like everything is normal, so can I.*

She headed for the table, pushing determinedly through the crowd of other high school students emerging with trays, and reached the back table in the corner covered in graffiti that the three of them had sat at every school day for the past two years.

"Hi, Florence," Felicity said, her eyes glued somewhere across the room. She shifted off to the side to get a better look while she pulled a plastic-wrapped sandwich out of her sack. "What's new?"

"You're kidding, right?" Florence demanded.

Felicity shifted her gaze over to her. "Oh, you mean Kendra."

"Yes, I mean Kendra!" Florence snapped. Then she quickly glanced around, and lowered her voice. "You know what she did. You know what she said. How can you be so calm about this?"

"Oh," Felicity said. "Well, we talked to the police."

"And they did *nothing,*" Florence hissed.

"Uh huh," Felicity said. "They said she's probably just brainwashed and will come back on her own."

"Do you really think someone could brainwash Kendra and keep her that way for days?" Florence demanded.

Felicity blinked. "Well, Dark Light was brainwashed for weeks before we saved her."

"That was Dark Light," Florence whispered, glancing around to make sure nobody was listening. Nobody was. She leaned forward. "This is Kendra. She has the strongest will of anybody I've ever met. There is no way she would stay brainwashed for that long."

"Okay," Felicity said. "So what do we do about Dark Kendra?"

Florence swallowed.

*Dark Kendra.* It was the obvious thing to call their teammate — brainwashed magical girls were traditionally called "Dark" before their name — but saying that felt like admitting that she was now their enemy.

*Don't be so sensitive,* Florence berated herself. *If you freak out about the idea now, what are you going to do when she comes back to attack both of you? Don't be stupid.*

Florence knew how it felt to be betrayed. And this time, she wouldn't freeze. This time, she wouldn't leave her friends in the lurch. Or *friend* — because she now only had Felicity. Kendra was their enemy.

She felt sick.

"I . . . I don't know," Florence said at last. "We still don't know if she was brainwashed, or if this was really her choice."

It was hard to believe that Kendra could be brainwashed for this long, but if she were, life would be much simpler. They'd save her, and everything would go back to normal.

Felicity looked puzzled. "But you just said —"

"I can have multiple opinions!" Florence snapped. "I'm as confused as you are!"

"I think I'm more confused, because you're confusing me," Felicity said.

Florence looked down at her tray. She traced her finger through the mashed potatoes. She picked at the tines of her plastic fork. She speared a noodle with it, then put the noodle back down again. "It didn't *seem* like she was brainwashed, but then why would she change like that?"

"Because she's brainwashed," Felicity said, as if it were obvious.

Florence bit her lip. Her mind flew to the final sight they'd seen of Kendra — when her best friend had been crying.

Brainwashed magical girls never looked like they were making heart-rending decisions. They looked supremely confident, certain that their new allegiances were not worth questioning. And yes, okay, it was extremely common for their focus items to change shape temporarily, but then so did their magical girl costumes. Kendra hadn't been transformed.

And even setting aside the fact that there was no way anyone could keep Kendra brainwashed for three days, who would have brainwashed her in the first place? They had beaten Queen Hemlock months ago. Sure, they still got attacked by stray leftover minions every now and then, but it seemed ludicrous that any of them might have access to brainwashing magic. If they had, they would have used it long before now.

And then there was the final issue . . .

"Either way," Florence said, "it's bizarre that she hasn't yet attacked us. I mean, after defection, usually the first thing —"

A pair of hands seized her arm.

"*Gasp!*" Felicity cried, saying the word rather than gasping. She was staring over Florence's shoulder with riveted attention. "Is Daniel looking at me?!"

Florence turned around and saw that, sure enough, the object of Felicity's stalker-crush was staring right in their direction.

"I hate your attention span," Florence muttered.

# The Lunchroom

Felicity's fingernails dug into her arm. "Eeeeek! What if he comes over? What if he asks me on a date? What if — what if — what if —?"

"What if you get your nails out of my arm?" Florence asked, trying to pry the painted claws out of her bicep.

"He's going to come over!!" Felicity squealed at full volume. "Daniel's going to come over here! He's going to tell me that he's passionately in love with me!"

Florence yanked her arm back, waited for the slightest loosening of fingernails, and then shoved Felicity with both arms. The girl's chair overbalanced, and she crashed to the floor.

"Hee hee hee, Daniel . . ." Felicity giggled, clutching her hands to her chest. She didn't seem to notice that she was now upside-down and had her brown ponytail spread across the floor.

Well, if Felicity could ignore that fact, so could she.

"Really, though, this situation is baffling," Florence said, digging a noodle out of her tray. She stared at it in concentration. "I can't think of any other reason but brainwashing, and yet . . ."

*Oh!* A thought struck her. *Blackmail!*

That would explain everything! The crying, the obvious regret, the fact that she hadn't been transformed, the fact that she hadn't yet attacked — everything!

Except for the halo growing spikes, anyway.

And the fact that it still begged the question of who could have blackmailed her.

And the fact that she could erase short-term memories, so it was unlikely she'd consider secrets leaking out to be a credible threat.

And one other, tiny thing . . .

Three years ago, shortly before they'd become magical girls, Florence clearly remembered watching TV with Kendra. A popular magical girl series had come on, called *Princess Prickly Pear.* ("The only magical girl with more spikes on her costume than her arch-nemesis!") That particular episode had revolved around her being blackmailed by some villain. Florence didn't remember the details, but she remembered that it had been a two-parter, and Kendra had blown up after the cliffhanger ending.

*"Seriously?!"* Kendra had shouted at the TV. *"Seriously?! How can you be so stupid? Go to the police!"*

Maybe Kendra would give in to blackmail. But it seemed a lot more likely that she'd pummel any villain who tried it and then go straight to the police to confess whatever she'd done so that no villain could use it against her again.

Besides, what kind of blackmail would Kendra consider a threat in the first place? Some crime she'd committed? Hardly likely. Social embarrassment? Kendra's interest in what strangers thought about her was humiliatingly low. Danger to her friends or family? That seemed the sort of thing that Kendra would respond to with answering violence without a second thought.

The thing about Kendra was, she was annoyingly straightforward. She always did what she thought was right, and sometimes what she thought was right was just outright *wrong*.

But you could trust Kendra to not give up for any reason, even if you really wanted her to.

*So blackmail,* Florence thought with a sigh, chewing on the tasteless noodle, *is almost certainly out.*

"Unless she has an evil boyfriend?" Florence blurted out, her head shooting up.

Yes! That would explain everything! Kendra's twisted sense of right and wrong might have gone totally haywire if she'd fallen in love with some villain! Florence's certainly had when she'd fallen in love with Lute Deathwave.

Florence cringed to remember it. She'd been an idiot and actually helped him commit two crimes. She'd also stood by helplessly while he'd attacked her teammates, who had come to stop him.

She didn't know if he had had true feelings for her, or if he'd been using her for the whole year they'd been dating before she'd learned that he was the son of their arch-nemesis. She liked to think that it had all been fake. He was in prison now, and it made it easier to try to forget him. She didn't know if she'd ever forgive him.

No matter how many sermons her father gave in church about the importance of forgiveness. He'd never been betrayed that way, after all.

# The Lunchroom

Florence swallowed her tasteless food. *She chewed me out about it when I fell for Dark Deathwave's son. She told me that I'd been a gullible idiot for believing his story about his family desperately needing those crystals to save his mom. She said that anyone who tells you to commit crimes should never be trusted, no matter what their reasons might be.*

Kendra saw things in black and white. Laws were good, and so were magical girls. Born mages were bad, and so were criminals. In Kendra's eyes, it would be hard to get much blacker than being a member of the Deathwave villain family.

Florence had tried to plead that he had always been nice to her, always been a perfect boyfriend, and okay, maybe he'd attacked them, but his reasoning had made so much sense —

To which Kendra had sarcastically responded, *"You're the one who's religious, Florence. That Garden of Eden story you believe in — do you really think the serpent didn't make sense?"*

Florence's stomach churned. There was nothing like being called on your own hypocrisy to realize just how much you'd strayed from the things you claimed to believe in.

So it was very clear where Kendra stood on the issue of evil boyfriends.

*Still . . .* Florence thought, *it has been two years since . . .*

*"No!"* Florence shouted, jumping up from her seat. She flung her arms out and glared at Felicity, as if her remaining teammate had been the one to suggest the idea. "My best friend is *not* a hypocrite!"

"Daniel . . ." Felicity replied in a dazed voice, looking across the lunchroom with no comprehension shown on her face.

"TWO WEEKS?!" Olivia shouted, slamming down the phone in fury. She spun around to face her husband, who was reading the newspaper in the kitchen way too calmly. "The police won't classify our daughter as a missing person for another *two weeks!*"

"I told you," he said, not looking up from the paper. "The usual window for a known magical girl is twenty days."

"That makes no sense!" she shouted.

Richard glanced over at her. "It makes perfect sense. That's the law because most missing magical girls return on their own before then."

"But Kendra's not 'most magical girls'!" Olivia cried, running her hands through her blonde hair. It was pulled up in several clips and hairpins. "She's more responsible!"

"Kendra's a teenager," Richard said flatly. "Who knows what she considers 'responsible.'"

Olivia fell silent. It would be different if their daughter had simply gone missing. She would have assumed that Kendra had been asked to save one of the millions of mascot worlds, or was off fighting evil somewhere else in their world without a phone. She would have worried, of course, but it was hard to worry too much when your daughter was a highly competent magical girl who had already defeated three arch-nemeses, even if she had remarked that she now wanted to find a fourth.

Olivia had never battled evil. The majority of magical girls didn't — only one-third even made powers to do so. She had been a singer, a mildly-successful flash-in-the-pan, dwarfed by other singing magical girls with more glitz or glamor or gimmicks within just a few months. Still, she had loved every minute of it, and she had kept her magical girl form for as long as possible before the magic had finally left.

She'd cried on that day in college when her focus item, the ring she wore on her finger all the time, had finally crumbled.

She missed the magic so much that she had gone into writing biographies of famous magical girls for her career. It wasn't the same as still having magic, but at least it was honoring something she loved intensely.

When Kendra had announced that she was going to be one, too, Olivia had been ecstatic. She'd helped Kendra design her costume, signed her up for all the classes she'd insisted she'd need, and bought her books and videos with how-to advice from all over the place. Kendra had absorbed it all like a sponge, using the same single-minded intensity she had had since the day she was born.

# The Lunchroom

Olivia had been a little disappointed, and very worried, when her twelve-year-old had announced that she wanted to be a fighting magical girl and battle evil. But she hadn't stood in her way, and by now, Olivia trusted her fifteen-year-old to be very good at it.

*So why?* Olivia thought, running her hands through her hair. *Why? Why did this happen?*

Florence had described the whole scene to them. It had sounded completely impossible, and yet, Olivia had seen no reason why Florence would lie. She had assumed, at first, that Kendra had simply been brainwashed. And yet it had been three days now, with no word.

"What if she really meant it?" Olivia fretted, speaking her greatest fear. She wrung her hands. "What if she really decided to become a . . . a . . . a . . ."

"A villain," Richard finished for her. "The word is 'villain.' And if she did, I'm sure we'll find out eventually. There's really nothing we can do about it right now."

"*Richard!*" Olivia exploded. "Our daughter's just turned *evil!*"

He looked up from his newspaper, looking rather annoyed. "No, she said she'd decided to become a villain. There might be a difference. There was with me."

Olivia fell silent. That was a subject they didn't bring up often. She knew that Richard had been a low-level minion for a Deathwave during his teenage years. In his rough neighborhood, he had had very few opportunities, and that had been the best-paying work for him to save up for college. He still claimed that he had no regrets.

Olivia felt very uncomfortable about that.

"Like what?" she asked, not wanting to get on that subject. "Fights with her friends? Wanting to lose her powers? None of those require defection!"

"True," her husband said, giving her a sneaky, crooked grin. "But you have to admit, this has more flair."

Olivia stared at him incredulously, but he just went back to his newspaper, flipping a page.

She turned and left the room in anger.

# Chapter 3
## The Upstairs

Verge squabbled with verge until Chronos couldn't take it any longer. She turned to head back up the stairs.

"Oh, no!" Kendra exclaimed, immediately disappearing from the squabble and appearing right in her way. "You're not getting away from me!"

Chronos sighed in exasperation. "Then why don't we *all* go upstairs?"

"Ooh!" the little girl who had introduced herself as Tiffany squealed before Kendra could respond. "I can go upstairs?!"

"N—" Kendra began.

The little girl burst past them, waving her wand wildly as she raced up the stairs. Bubbles shot from the wand and wobbled in the air behind her. "Yay! I haven't seen the upstairs in *years!*"

"Good job," Kendra said sourly.

"I don't believe in keeping people trapped," Chronos shrugged.

"*You* may not," Kendra said, folding her arms, "but *I* believe in prisons for people who deserve them."

"That's not a very villainish thing to say," Chronos said.

Kendra glared at her.

Chronos headed up the stairs after the excited little girl. The middle floor was filled with bubbles, spinning in circles and floating up to the high ceiling with the tall chandelier. Despite the clouds of semitransparent spheres, it was still easy to pick out the little girl. She was racing around, a blur of colors that more and more bubbles were emanating from.

Chronos was a little amused. Also, she wondered how many more powers the little girl was hiding. The ability to produce bubbles at a moment's notice didn't seem very dangerous, but for all she knew, the same power could produce explosions.

"Can I sleep in a real bedroom now? Huh? Huh? Huh?" the little girl cried, spinning around. Bubbles whirled in a spiral.

"Wouldn't you . . . rather go home to your family?" Chronos asked awkwardly.

The little girl stopped.

All the bubbles in the room popped.

"Nooooooooooooooooooo!" the little girl howled, flinging herself to the floor. "Please don't make me go back! I'll do anything!"

Chronos's mouth opened, astonished. She'd had serious problems with her family, enough that she had left and never gone back once she'd reached the age of eighteen, but this kind of reaction from a child seemed ridiculous.

"What's wrong with your family?" she managed to ask.

"My aunt and uncle *hate* me!" the little girl wailed, picking herself up off the floor. Huge tears welled up in her eyes. "Even my cousin doesn't care one bit!"

*An orphan,* Chronos realized. *She must be an orphan.* "You mean they're the only family you've got?"

The little girl hung her head, sniffling. "And they think I'm dead. I saw my funeral years ago. No one even cried at it."

"But that's impossible!" Chronos burst out. "You must have had friends! Teammates?"

That last word was a mistake.

"My teammates didn't want me, either!" the little girl wailed. "Their moms *made* them include me 'cause I didn't have any friends!"

Chronos shuddered. She knew how it felt to not have any friends. Her older sister had made sure of that.

A derisive snort came from behind them. Chronos turned, and Kendra was heading up the stairs.

She walked through the door and planted herself right next to the little girl. "Clearly you should have chosen a better team."

The little girl let out a loud howl and collapsed onto the floor in sobs again.

"Kendra —" Chronos began.

"Crocodile tears," Kendra shot back. "She's playing for sympathy, and you're letting her. If she's a verge at the age of ten, she has to be an awful person. The magic system's really merciful to girls that young. If she can't transform anymore, she has to be a much worse person than I am."

Chronos was so offput by Kendra referring to herself that way that she couldn't find a response.

"I'm not a bad person!" the little girl sobbed. "I just want to be happy! Nobody ever loved me outside! Only my machine-friends understand me!"

Chronos winced.

*"Nobody loves you more than I do, Chronos,"* ten-year-old Rhea had said once, patting her hair. *"I'm the only one who understands you."*

Chronos shuddered, wishing she could exorcise the memories of her vile sister's mind games.

If anyone had tried to force Chronos to go back home to the parents who had done nothing about her older sister, to the stifling traditions of Olympus Estates, to Great-Uncle Nico with his stranglehold on the entire extended family, she would have screamed far more vehemently than this.

No. Anyone, even a young child, deserved the freedom to go or leave.

"I'm sorry, Tiffany," Chronos said quietly. "You don't have to go back home. You're free to go wherever you want."

"Wherever I want?" the little girl asked, her face peeking up from behind her hands.

Chronos nodded.

"Wherever I want, to live?" the little girl asked tremulously.

Chronos nodded again.

# The Upstairs

In a flash, the little girl was halfway up the staircase to the top floor. "Dibs on the biggest bedroom!"

"*Crocodile tears!*" Kendra snarled.

Chronos set her jaw. She didn't care. It didn't really matter who the little girl was. If she didn't want to go home to her family, she wasn't going to force her.

"I'm going to take this one!" a voice shouted from upstairs. A door slammed. "No, wait, this one!" Another door slammed. "No, wait, this one!"

"Great job, soothsayer," Kendra growled. "Now we'll never get rid of her."

"What are you talking about?" Chronos asked defensively. "She's not staying! She just misunderstood that she can go *anywhere*. She's been a prisoner here. Of course she won't want to stay —"

A head with blonde pigtails poked over the top of the wall beside the stairs. "Oh, by the way, Davie the Defense Grid only listens to me! No one can kick me out but me!"

Chronos stopped abruptly, her thoughts screeching to a halt.

The little girl raced off again. "Ooh, Boris the Broom! I haven't upgraded you in *ages!*"

"She could have escaped at any time," Kendra grated. "In no way was that kid ever really a prisoner."

Chronos swallowed.

She looked at Kendra. Kendra looked at her.

"I'm going back home," Chronos announced, heading toward the stairs. It almost didn't matter that the former magical girl would inevitably follow her. Better to have one pest constantly in her hair than two.

"You can't leave me alone with that girl!" Kendra said indignantly, pointing upward. "She's *crazy!*"

The little girl's voice echoed from upstairs as she continued to race from room to room. "Hi, Stevie the Shower! Hi, Linus the Light Bulb! *WHOA!!* Robbie the Rocket Pack!"

"Indeed," Chronos said. "And you still haven't given me a convincing reason to stay."

She headed determinedly up the stairs.

For once, Kendra didn't teleport in front of her. Instead, the former magical girl marched up the stairs behind her. "Saving the *world?*"

"Couldn't care less," Chronos said, not turning around.

"Responsibility towards her?" Kendra said accusingly.

"She's in *your* lair. She's *your* problem."

"Then responsibility towards *me!*" Kendra shouted.

Chronos spun around in fury. "I never asked you to turn villain! You chose your own path, despite my clearly telling you not to do something exactly like this! I will not let you choose my path for me!"

Kendra marched up the stairs, her feet slamming into the floor with every step. "So you thought it was okay to show up, call my whole life 'propaganda,' then just casually *leave?*"

"It wasn't casual!" Chronos said. "It was the most difficult thing I've done in years! And now I'm done with it!"

"How nice for you," Kendra said furiously, storming up another few stairs. "How nice that you can blithely throw a bomb into somebody else's life and just walk away."

Chronos swallowed. When she put it that way . . .

"I . . . I wasn't trying to convince you to quit." Chronos hesitated, knowing that that was probably a lie. Kendra's quitting magic would have been the easiest solution. "I just hoped to end the nightmares."

"So what are you planning to do next time someone gives you bad dreams?" Kendra demanded.

Chronos fell silent. She had no answer to that question.

Nightmares, the most extreme of futures, had been her constant companion for most of her life.

She'd dreamt about the revolution in Mágico.

She'd dreamt about her parents' deaths.

She'd dreamt about two moon shuttle crashes, neither of which had happened.

She'd dreamt about the Spikewallow gang in Melbourne.

She'd dreamt about hundreds of battles between the *tienlong* and the *kamikaze.*

Futures that later happened, futures that soon ceased to be possibilities . . . it didn't matter. They all littered her dreams.

There had never been a solution to that problem.

Ever.

"That's why you should stay," Kendra said, arriving at the top of the stairs. She leaned against the bannister and looked at Chronos. "Next time you're afraid of someone, tell me, and I'll fix the problem. You stay a hermit, you sleep at night, and I save the world."

Chronos was silent.

There was no doubt that, if another future catastrophe arose, it would show up to haunt her dreams.

There was no doubt that all of Kendra's future allies were still around. Any one of them could choose to go down the same path without her.

Dulcina Caramelo. Namikaze Tateru. Jeanne d'Rouen. Princesa.

There was also the fact that Chronos didn't know for certain whether Avenging Angel was truly gone. Escaping and getting far away from Kendra would never change that fact. Because she had been so important to Kendra's past, any extreme paths that were in her future were bound to have Chronos in them.

If nothing else, if Kendra turned into Avenging Angel, her first course of action would be to kill Chronos.

And she still had the watch.

Chronos breathed in and out. It wasn't just that Kendra had a point. Everything obvious was pointing her in one direction.

"Well . . ." Chronos said slowly, hardly able to voice the words.

A blur of fire roared past them. Chronos leapt back, and the crazy little girl zoomed up to the ceiling, wearing a rocket pack. Amazingly, her legs weren't burned despite the huge tails of fire blazing out the back. She had to be protected magically.

"Wheeeeeeeeeeeeeeeeee!" the crazy little girl screamed.

"Fine," Chronos said abruptly, shoulders hunching. She jabbed her finger in the direction the small lunatic was heading. "*You* save the world, and *you* take care of that thing."

"I'm not a thing!" the little girl shouted, crashing into a wall. "My name's Tiffany!"

They spent the next few hours moving all of Chronos's things out of her apartment in Athens and into a bedroom that was very small and crammed into a corner on the east side of the building. It had a cracked outer wall, and the window was filthy.

"This is a terrible room," Kendra opined. "There are no shade trees, and it's in full sun. It'll be really hot in the morning. You should sleep on the west side, like I am."

Chronos smiled. That was the reason she wanted this room. It was the farthest away from Kendra's.

"FIX IT!" was Tiffany's only opinion.

The cracks in the wall mended themselves.

The window stayed filthy.

Kendra was extremely grumpy when she discovered there were no cleaning supplies anywhere in Chronos's things.

Overall, the moving went extremely quickly due to Kendra's ability to teleport everything, even large furniture, into whatever place she wanted it. Despite the fact that Chronos had agreed to stay, she still didn't let Chronos or Tiffany anywhere near the watch, so she did most of the work of moving herself.

At last, the only things remaining were Tiffany's many piles of clutter down in the dungeons.

"Now you can help me!" Tiffany said excitedly. "I have Matty the Mattress, and Benny the Boxes, and Barry the Bars from the cages —"

"Pass," Kendra said. "I've got things to do."

Chronos frowned. "What kind of things?"

"None of your beeswax," the former magical girl said.

And then she teleported away.

Chronos let out an annoyed grunt. *Why couldn't she have done that when I wanted to get rid of her?*

Without Kendra, moving Tiffany out of the dungeons took far more work. The mattress alone took nearly an hour to get up the stairs and into the biggest bedroom, which Tiffany had, in fact, claimed. And then there were dozens of heavy boxes filled with odds and ends and lots of strange machinery. And dozens more piles of toys and heaps of clothing.

# The Upstairs

"Where did you even *get* all of these things?" Chronos demanded incredulously as the little girl brought another armload of ruffled clothing upstairs. "You were a prisoner!"

"Clyde the Clothing Cupboard wasn't my idea," Tiffany said, her expression shifty. "Or Tom the Toybox. Or Porter the Poster Tube."

Chronos rubbed her forehead. She was going to have to get rid of all of those things, as well as the refrigerator, just as soon as she figured out how to destroy the brainwasher.

# Chapter 4
## The Bedroom

Jumbled and confused thoughts warred through Florence's mind as she walked home.

*Did Kendra really quit being a magical girl?* she wondered. *Do I want to quit being a magical girl?*

Without Kendra, there really wasn't much point to Wings of Justice. Without their team leader, Green Fairy and Pink Dragon were just ordinary magical girls who had good powers but no ambitions.

*Which is probably a good thing,* Florence reminded herself. *You hated the way Kendra kept trying to plan your future for you.*

Which was true . . . it was absolutely true . . . and yet . . .

Kendra had always had a very clear vision of what she wanted. She had always lain out clear paths that she expected everybody else to follow. It had driven Florence crazy, but reacting to those paths she didn't want had at least given her direction.

Without Kendra to annoy her into knowing what she *didn't* want to do next, Florence felt lost.

Not to mention that she missed her best friend.

*Dissolve the team . . .* she thought, walking slowly down the sidewalk as she passed by a playground. The same playground where her best friend had been seen crying the day before she'd vanished. *Kendra, why would you dissolve the team?*

# The Bedroom

Florence looked around for clues, but there was nothing telling. Just a bunch of kids on teeter totters, swings, and climbing up to slide down the slide.

*Why would you quit?* Florence thought. *Why would you defect like that? What HAPPENED?*

If only she'd had some clue, she could at least have decided on her next step. She could have chosen to fight Kendra, or save her, or trust her to handle things herself. But given that she now knew nothing, it felt like all she could do was abandon her.

*I just don't understand . . .* Florence thought morosely.

She reached her house, a small, one-story building, and pushed the front door open. She passed the living room, where her father had a Bible, sheets of paper, and several other books spread out in front of him. It looked like he was preparing his sermon for Sunday.

"Hi, Dad," Florence called, waving.

He glanced up and smiled and waved, then tapped his pen against the table for a few seconds. His eyes brightened, and he scribbled a line on the piece of paper in front of him.

"Flo! Flo! Flo! Flo!" Jacob called, running down the hallway. "Dad said we could shoot hoops after I finished my homework and you got home from track! Catch!"

His hands whipped out from behind his back, and a basketball came flying at her. Florence caught it instinctively.

"He shoots . . . he scores!" Jacob yelled.

"Jacob, I told you, no throwing things in the house!" their mother called from the kitchen, where it sounded like she was chopping up vegetables.

Florence swallowed a lump in her throat. Everything seemed so . . . normal around her house. Even though her world outside the family was shattering. Even though her best friend was missing, and her team was gone.

In some ways, it was comforting to know that her family was stable while everything else seemed to be shattering around her. In other ways, it was maddening. Why weren't they all as devastated as she currently felt?

"Florence," her mother said, sounding concerned. She set down the knife and came walking out into the hallway. "Are you okay?"

"No," Florence said shortly. She didn't explain. She didn't think she should have to.

"If you need to talk, we're here," her mother said. "If you don't need to talk, we're here, too."

Florence nodded, blinking back tears. She didn't want to talk right now. She definitely didn't want to play basketball. She just wanted to go into her room and be alone.

"Come on, Jacob," her mother said. "I'll play basketball with you. Paul! Come play, too!"

Her father's voice called, "But I'm in the middle of —"

"That can wait!" her mother called. "We're losing daylight!"

There was a shuffling of papers, and then Florence's father emerged from the living room. He rubbed his eyes, then rubbed his bald head. He hated his hair, so he kept his scalp shaved.

"Do you want to join us?" he asked Florence.

She shook her head.

He nodded, and then all three of her family members headed outside. Soon, there were shouts of laughter from her brother and the sound of the basketball thumping and feet scrambling across the driveway.

Florence breathed a sigh of relief. It was nice to be alone. She closed her eyes, turned the doorknob to her room, and stepped inside.

"Hi, Florence," a voice said.

Florence's eyes flew open. Sitting on her bed, as casually as if it were nothing, was Kendra.

Florence's mouth fell open. She let out an incoherent, high-pitched, "Urghha!"

"What took you so long?" Kendra continued. "I've been waiting here for nearly an hour. You usually get home from track much sooner than this."

"*KENDRA!*" Florence exclaimed, dropping her backpack. It thudded to the ground.

"Yep."

"You — what — why — where have you *been?!*" Florence sputtered.

"Turning villain," Kendra said calmly. "Just like I said I would. Did you think I was lying?"

"You . . . but . . . *WHY?*"

Kendra shrugged.

Florence couldn't process this. It was unreasonable. It was unthinkable. It was unbelievable.

It was so very, very Kendra.

"Who brainwashed you?" Florence blurted out.

"I wasn't brainwashed," Kendra said, crossing her legs. Her foot hit a stuffed duffel bag that Florence noticed, for the first time, was sitting on the floor beside her. "Sorry."

"Then where have you *been?!*" Florence exclaimed.

"I was turning *villain,*" Kendra said, rolling her eyes. "Duhhh."

Florence leaned forward and clenched her hands into fists. Her best friend was the most annoying person on the planet. "KENDRA!! EXPLAIN!!"

"It's . . . complicated." Kendra hunched her knees up to her chest. "I kind of had to do it. To save the world."

Florence stared at her blankly.

"I didn't want to quit," Kendra said, tracing her finger in a circle around the knee of her jeans. "I really didn't want to defect. But . . . I found out . . . it's possible for magical girls to turn corrupt. One with sufficient charisma and arrogance could even lead the world to destruction. That would have been my future. A born mage showed me. So I . . ."

"You listened to a *born mage?*" Florence exploded. "After all the things you said to me about Lute Deathwave? Are you crazy? *Obviously* he was lying!"

"No, she wasn't!" Kendra snapped. Her feet stomped back on the floor, and she planted an accusing finger forward. "I became a villain for the same reason we both became magical girls: to protect world peace!"

Florence stared at her best friend dumbly.

This was Kendra. This was definitely Kendra. Only Kendra could be so ridiculously certain about something that made no sense whatsoever.

It wasn't a brainwashed version.  It wasn't a blackmailed version.  It didn't even seem to be a crazy-in-love version.  It was just . . . somehow . . . her best friend, having made a mind-bogglingly stupid decision that she seemed determined to justify.

But if she wasn't here to apologize, wasn't here to come back, there was only one reason she would have returned.

"Kendra . . ." Florence said slowly, preparing to summon her focus item, " . . . why are you here?"

"Because you're my best friend," Kendra said.

She reached out her hand.  It hung in the air for several silent seconds.

"Will you trust me?  Will you join me?" she said.

Florence stared at her in incomprehension.

"Join me in being a villain," Kendra said.  "Join my new team. Join me in saving the world."

Florence's eyes widened and widened.

An unfathomable chasm stretched between them.  A chasm filled with all that had been, all that ever could have been, all that never would be.

Florence took a step backwards.  "Dad's always taught me that right and wrong . . ."

A spark of flame appeared at her wrist, and then spread into a swirl of fire going past her elbow.  It had never done that before, but she barely spared a thought for it.

" . . . are more important than friendship."

She had made the wrong decision with Lute Deathwave. She would not make the same mistake with Kendra.

Now wearing her focus item, Florence lifted her arms high. "Pink Dragon . . . *flare!*"

She whooshed up to the ceiling, spinning around at a fast rate, flames burning away her clothing as her dozens of braids expanded and coiled into corkscrew curls at the bottom.  Enormous bat wings burst from her back as the flames blossomed outward into a fluffy pink dress, a style that she had been in love with at twelve years old.

She landed, flames roaring around her.  They swirled and sucked into her bracelet like a vortex.

"I'm trying to save the world, Flo," Kendra sighed, leaning forward. "What part of that don't you understand?"

"What part?!" Florence sputtered. "What part *does* make sense? You know what villains are like, Kendra!"

"Of course I know what villains are like," Kendra said. There was a strange gleam in her eyes. "What I didn't understand was what magical girls are like. I didn't understand that we weren't all virtuous."

*Well, duh!* Florence thought. *I've been trying to tell you that for years! Just because somebody has magical girl powers doesn't mean they're automatically perfect! You have to use good judgment apart from that!*

"That's why I have to be a villain," Kendra said. The gleam was back in her eyes. "I have to purify the magic system. I have to cut out anyone who's corrupt."

"You have to *not be a villain!*" Florence shouted. "Are you listening to yourself? You sound nuts!"

"It doesn't matter," Kendra said, shaking her head. "Any cost is worth it to save the world. That's what I'm doing."

"By becoming a *villain?*" Florence snapped incredulously. She swung her bracelet around to face Kendra. The bracelet that could turn her breath into a stream of fire, ice, or poison as soon as she wished it.

Kendra let out a snort. "All right. I'll leave. I'm sorry I came."

Showing no fear whatsoever, she lifted up the blinds behind the bed and unlocked the window.

"But . . . your parents," Florence said, pulling her arm back. "Felicity?"

"No way," Kendra said, rolling her eyes. "If you don't understand, there's no chance they will."

Florence shoved her left arm out, turning her wrist to the right so that the blue gem that created ice was on top. "I'll breathe ice at you!" she threatened. "I'll *make* you stay and face them!"

Kendra paid no attention. She just hopped down to the floor, picked up the duffel bag, and heaved it through the window.

"I will!" Florence cried.

"Just ice?" Kendra asked sardonically, sitting on the edge of the window to hop out. "Why don't you breathe fire or poison, while you're at it? I'm a villain. The law justifies killing me."

Florence cringed. Of course she wasn't going to kill Kendra. She knew perfectly well that ice was safe. They'd used it on dozens of minions to turn them in to the police.

That was exactly what she should do.

But she didn't move.

Somehow, even if Kendra was betraying her . . . she couldn't bring herself to betray Kendra. Using her magic on her best friend and former teammate would feel like a betrayal.

*Turn the other cheek,* Florence thought slowly, pulling her arm back in. *Return good for evil.*

"Pulling back?" Kendra taunted. "Don't you know I'm a dangerous criminal?"

Florence swallowed. "But . . . then . . . why don't you attack *me?*"

Kendra stared at her in disbelief. "Duh. You're my best friend. You'll never be my enemy."

Fire roared around Florence as she detransformed. Her bat wings slurped back into her back, and her fluffy pink dress dissolved into smoke that coiled back into her former clothes.

"Go," Florence said quietly. "I won't attack you, either."

"Thanks," Kendra said. "I hope we'll be on the same side again someday."

She swung her legs through the open window and dropped to the ground.

Florence ran to the window to watch which way Kendra was heading, but all she caught was a few traces of fading sparkles.

*Teleportation,* Florence realized. *Like she did before. How did Kendra get that power?*

Perhaps she'd never know. Because this might be the last conversation they'd ever have.

"Yeah," Florence said sadly. "Me, too."

www.ingramcontent.com/pod-product-compliance
Lightning Source LLC
Chambersburg PA
CBHW022044050726
47591CB00003B/947